Mica is a very naughty girl who lives with her mom and dad. Mica loves running around her house, throwing pillows and breaking ornaments she finds around her

Mica doesn't like to share her toys with anyone but she loves to take the toys which belong to her friends when they are playing

Mica's mom told her to behave but she only got tantrums.

Outside on the streets, a truck is heading fast to the zoo, carrying some cages with animals in them. Suddenly, a ball hits one of the cages and makes it fall out of the truck. The cages breaks and Mico comes out of it, a small and naughty monkey who starts running happily around the streets

From the top of a tree Micco sees a room full of toys and, with much curiosity, decides to go

When he gets into the room he finds himself surprised with all the toys around. All of a sudden the door opens and Mica comes into the room, jumping of joy for seeing Mico

Mica thinks Mico is a new gift from her parents so runs towards him and hugs him tight and she tells him: "I will name you Garbanzo"

Mico is very happy to receive all this love so he starts playing with a teddy bear in the room but Mica sees him and tells him: "This is mine Garbanzo, you can't play with it" as she takes the Teddy bear out of his hands. Mico, playful, pulls it back but Mica, very mad as she doesn't want to share her toys pulls it back again and yells: " I have told you this is mine"

Mico, furious, takes the teddy bear out of Mica's hands and starts running fastly around the house. Mica chases him desperately

Mico jumps from one place to another leaving Mica far behind. Mica lays on the floor very tired and Mico approaches to her as he hugs the teddy bear

Mica takes Mico for a walk in a baby carriage, him and the teddy bear are sitting very comfortable within it

A lady approaches curios and observes Mico " what a weird toy" she says. Mico stands up and sticks his tongue out to her. The lady goes away scared of him

Mico and Mica walk down the street. Across the road a fruit seller pulls his fruit car. Mico jumps out of the baby carriage and is ready to run towards it. Mica pulls him by his tails and tells him " No Garbanzo, we can't cross the road alone" Mico tries to scale but Mica is holding him strongly. Desperate Mico starts crying and makes a tantrum

Mica can't stand the tantrum anymore so she releases him. Mico crossed the road chasing the fruit seller. Mica yells at him worried " Garbanzo come back" but Mico won't listen .

Mico jumps over the fruit car and pulls a banana. The fruit seller tries to catch him but Mico dodges him several times until, without noticing it, he catches Mico from one of his legs

Panaderia
Mico hits him precisely on his Head with the teddy bear and managed to related himself but when he is ready to scape the fruit seller catches him back again, from his neck and tells him " got you this time little thief"

nadería
All of a sudden Mica bites one of the legs of the fruit seller who cries out in pain. Mica and Mico try to scape but the seller managed to catch them

The bell rings at Mica'a house. Mica's das open the door as he watches
surprised the fruit seller holding Mica in one hand and Mico in the other
one : " are these two yours" the fruit seller asks him

The door closes. Mica's dad looks at them both surprised and ask Mica " can I know who is this one" pointing at Mico. Mica replies: he is garbanzo and I found him in the room . " what do you mean garbanzo" her dad replies " who is responsible of all this problem" Mica and Mico reply by pontine to each other

The bell rings again and at the door is the zoo keeper who very worried asks

"Excuse sir have you seen ...." Mico sees him and runs to hug him

Mico and the zookeeper are ready to go "Go on mico say goodbye" he tells Mico. Mico approaches Mica and gives her back the teddy bear but Mica gives it back with a smile and tells him "Take it Mico it's yours now "

Mico hugs Mica tight and jumps happily

Mica's mom and dad wave goodbye to the zoo truck which goes away on the road

When they go into the house Mica
wasn't there so very worried they start
searching around the house "Mica,
Mica"

They get into Mica's bedroom and find her deep sleep. Very surprised they leave the room and leave quitely. They leave her to rest from a day that she will never forget from all the lessons learnt

www.ingramcontent.com/pod-product-compliance
Lightning Source LLC
Chambersburg PA
CBHW042018110726
48006CB00004B/1136